Christmas Tree Memories

by Aliki

HarperCollinsPublishers

With thanks to Nancy Christoff
for the spark

The illustrations for this book were done on watercolor board, using a combination of
ink, watercolors, and pencil crayons.

Christmas Tree Memories   Copyright © 1991 by Aliki Brandenberg   Printed in the U.S.A.   All rights reserved.
1   2   3   4   5   6   7   8   9   10   First Edition

Library of Congress Cataloging-in-Publication Data   Aliki.   Christmas tree memories /
written and illustrated by Aliki.   p.   cm.
Summary: Family members admire the ornaments on their Christmas tree and share their memories of previous
holidays as evoked by the ornaments.   ISBN 0-06-020007-3. — ISBN 0-06-020008-1
(lib. bdg.)   [1. Christmas—Fiction.   2. Christmas trees—Fiction.]   I. Title.
PZ7.A397Ch   1991   90-45575   [E]—dc20   CIP   AC

Merry Christmases
to
John Locke Marshall

TINNG. TINNG.
The children heard the bell.
It was the signal.
They peeked through the half-open door.
There stood the tree, glowing with candles,
its branches heavy with decorations.

Tomorrow—Christmas Day—they would tiptoe down to
the pine-scented room to see what presents Santa had brought.
But tonight—as always on Christmas Eve—this family sat
before the tree, sharing memories.

Some of the ornaments were older than the children.
But most of them the family had made,
some together with friends.
Each brought back a memory.

There is my heart of dough.

You were only two when you made it.
That was the year of the blizzard. Remember?

There was no water or electricity, and we boiled
snow for the soup and told stories by the fire.

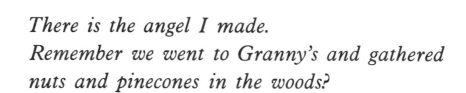

There is the angel I made.
Remember we went to Granny's and gathered
nuts and pinecones in the woods?

Then we went home and baked cookies.
And I made the walnut cradle.

Aunt Eunice brought an ornament every year.
She brought the lion and the lamb when you
were just babies.

Then she got sick and died, but I remember her.

Remember we made "stained-glass" cookies
in kindergarten, and the mice escaped and ate
most of them up?

One year it was origami.
A lady at the museum showed us
how to fold paper into all kinds of shapes.

We made spool figures the time we had chicken pox.

We made a tent over our beds, and you brought us hot soup and sage tea.

We learned about corn that year.
Jolly showed us how to make wreaths from husks
when we all went to the country together.

Then we strung cranberries, and baby Nell sat on them.

And we all painted eggs.

Bobby gave us his but it broke
and you glued it together.

There's Bobby's starfish Santa.

*Remember the summer we went diving
and collecting shells?*

You made a mobile from them.

That year I banged my sled into a tree
and was bandaged like a mummy.

And you learned to crochet decorations like Esther.

There's the fish we made of candle drips,
with Steve and May that New Year's Eve.
We woke you to see the fireworks,
but the next day you didn't remember.

The rocking horse is from Aunt Ann and Uncle Peter.

*Remember the summer at Yiayia and Papouli's
when Cousin Gregory lost his tooth in a pillow fight?*

*Papouli whittled the drum for me and the bell for you.
He made the best spaghetti sauce!*

The candles blinked and died out, one by one.
They sat in the dark, quiet with their thoughts.

Santa's almost here.
And tomorrow everyone is coming
for Christmas lunch.
We'd better get to bed.

They climbed the stairs.

Did you leave a snack for Santa?

Yes, and one for Nefi.

Good night, they said.

Merry Christmas! Good night.
Good memories!

Yes. Good, beautiful memories.
They fell asleep thinking of them still—
and of what new memories tomorrow might bring.

Copyright © 2003 by Nord-Süd Verlag AG, Gossau Zürich, Switzerland
First published in Switzerland under the title *Leonardos grosser Traum*.
English translation copyright © 2004 by North-South Books Inc., New York

First published in the United States, Great Britain, Canada, Australia, and New Zealand in 2004
by North-South Books, an imprint of Nord-Süd Verlag AG, Gossau Zürich, Switzerland.
Distributed in the United States by North-South Books Inc., New York.

Library of Congress Cataloging-in-Publication Data is available.
A CIP catalogue record for this book is available from The British Library.
ISBN 0-7358-1926-2 (trade edition)
1 3 5 7 9 HC 10 8 6 4 2
ISBN 0-7358-1927-0 (library edition)
1 3 5 7 9 LE 10 8 6 4 2
Printed in Switzerland

For more information about our books, and the authors and artists
who create them, visit our web site: www.northsouth.com

Hans de Beer

LEONARDO'S DREAM

Translated by Marisa Miller

North-South Books
New York / London

Leonardo the penguin lived at the South Pole. He looked a bit different from the other penguins because *his* beak was yellow and theirs were red. But none of them seemed to care about that, so Leonardo didn't either. What Leonardo *did* care about was that he couldn't fly, for flying was Leonardo's greatest dream.

Every day, Leonardo would smile confidently at his wings and whisper, "You'll be big soon, and then . . ." He would stand on one leg at the top of the cliff, letting the wind brush through his feathers, and imagine that he was flying over the ocean. It made him very happy.

"My friends call me Leo," Leonardo told everyone who passed by. But the truth was that he had no friends.

The other penguins thought he was a strange bird because they had never felt the slightest desire to fly. Leonardo, on the other hand, showed no interest in swimming, which is what penguins do best.

Day after day, he watched birds soaring overhead. And day after day, he checked to see if his wings had grown at all. They hadn't, but that didn't stop him. He hopped and flapped and hopped and flapped, but it was no use. He never left the ground.

The other penguins made fun of Leonardo's dream of flying. One day they walked past him laughing. "What's the matter—bad flying weather?" they teased.

"What do you know about flying weather!" Leonardo shouted back. He would even fly in a blizzard, he thought bravely—if he could fly at all.

Despite their taunts, Leonardo worked on his daily flight exercises but soon gave up. "Definitely not flying weather," he admitted sadly.

The next day, Leonardo saw a bird with long, slender wings and a yellow beak soaring silently in the sky. He had never seen a bird fly so beautifully. When the bird landed close by, Leonardo went running up to him. "I'm Leo," he said, out of breath, "may I please look at your wings?"

"But of course," said the bird, surprised. "I'm Otto Albatross," he added, and unfolded his unbelievably long wings.

"When I grow up, my wings will be that big too," declared Leonardo.

"Well, Leo," said Otto, kindly, "that might take a few years."

A few years! No! Leonardo wanted to fly right here,
right now! He examined Otto's wings very carefully, then
rushed to the shore. There, he gathered as many sticks as
he could find and carried them to an open field.

Curious, Otto glided down from a cliff. At Leonardo's
request, Otto opened his wings wide. Leonardo studied
them once more, then began to set out the sticks he
had collected. Otto was amazed when he saw what the
little penguin had in mind.

Finally Leonardo was finished. "Look at my new wings!" he cried. "Just my size!"

"Do you really think they will work?" asked Otto, doubtfully.

But Leonardo wasn't discouraged. He was certain that with the new wings he could finally fly. He waddled bravely to the cliff and peered down. He was feeling a little queasy, but when a gentle breeze ruffled his feathers, Leonardo breathed deeply, took a running start, and . . .

. . . crashed right into a snowdrift!

"What happened?" he asked, digging himself out of the powdery snow.

"Are you okay, Leo?" asked Otto.

"I am, but my new wings aren't," replied Leonardo. "Come down here and see what I landed on."

They dug through the deep snow.

"Leo!" said Otto, astonished. "That looks like a flying machine! You wouldn't have found it if it hadn't been for those crazy wings of yours," he added, laughing.

   As evening neared, the wind picked up and swirled the snow around. Leonardo and Otto had to work hard to free the flying machine.

   "Wow!" said Otto. "It's not the latest model, but it's in good condition."

   "In good condition? Oh, Otto, do you think that maybe we could . . ." Leonardo asked.

   "We'll see tomorrow, Leo," the albatross replied. "I'm so tired I can hardly stand."

   Leonardo was exhausted too, but he was so excited that it took him a long time to fall asleep.

The next morning Leonardo cleared out the cockpit and found a flying cap, goggles, and a scarf. Now he looked like a real pilot! He also found a flight manual and studied the instructions carefully.

Meanwhile, Otto busied himself with the propeller. The motor rattled, clattered, and clanged . . . and started! "Hurray!" Otto cheered, stomping the ground with his big feet.

Suddenly, penguins came from every direction, curious to see what all the excitement was about.

Otto called out to them, "All aboard! Fasten your seat belts!"

The penguins hopped onto the wings.

"Spread out evenly," Otto commanded. He turned to Leonardo. "Don't worry, I'll help you!" he said with a wink.

"Get ready for takeoff!" Leonardo shouted.

First, the plane jerked and jolted, rocked and shook, then slowly it began to roll. Faster and faster it went until it lifted off the ground! They were airborne! Leonardo was flying!

"You did it, Leo! You're flying! Isn't it wonderful?" cried Otto.

"It's fantastic!" Leonardo shouted back. "I'm flying over the sea. I'm flying!"

All too soon Otto said, "We'd better head back. There's not much fuel in the tank."

As soon as the flying machine had touched down, the motor began to sputter and the propeller came to a stop.

"That was a perfect landing," declared Otto. "But, Leo, it was also your first and last flight. The fuel is gone."

That didn't bother Leonardo. He was overjoyed—his dream had come true.

A cheer rose from the crowd: "Bravo, Leo! You really did it! Hooray! Hooray!"

Leonardo's perseverance had made his dream of flying come true, and he worked just as hard learning how to swim. The other penguins were very proud of him, and from then on they called him Leo. When Otto stopped by for a visit, Leonardo showed him how he could leap into the water from the cliff.

"Now you're really flying!" said Otto, admiringly.

"Yes, but this time I'm using my very own swimming wings," replied Leonardo laughing.